Stacey Became a Frog One Day

HUGGINS
FAMILY

Candelaria Norma Silva

To request permission, contact the publisher at author@candelarianormasilva.com.

Hardcover: 978-1-7351385-1-0
Paperback: 978-1-7351385-0-3
Ebook: 978-1-7351385-2-7

Library of Congress Number: 2020909636

First edition October 2020.

Cover design and illustrations by Justin Deocampo Aquidado

Published By Candelaria Norma Silva
Boston, Massachusetts USA

http://candelarianormasilva.com

This book is dedicated to my children and my grandchildren:

Saige

Tommie

Amber

Cyrus

Everyone who's encouraged me

You, too (Maddie, Unique, Darian, Dionna, and Leanne)

And to my beloved husband, Tessil.

Thank You

Thank you to the parents, grandparents, teachers, aunts, uncles, childcare professionals, cousins, and others who purchase this book and will read it aloud to children. As an appreciation of your support, you can download a free coloring page from *Stacy Became A Frog One Day* at **http://candelarianormasilva.com**

You have been an unexpected angel, and said you could help me get my children's books published. Thank you to Delanda Coleman, author, and principal of Sydney and Coleman. You have been an exemplary consultant, an encouraging but firm taskmaster. This is the first of several books we'll make happen together. Your book, *More than a Princess*, should be on every young girl's shelf. You can learn more about her books at **http://SydneyandColeman.com**

A picture book requires illustrations that make sense for the story and help it sing. Thank you to Justin for being patient through all of the drafts. Check out his D&D related illustrations & resources that you can download for free on his Patreon website:
Printable Tabletop Things in this **url: http://bitly.ws/93c7**

If you'd like a signed copy of *Stacy Became A Frog One Day*, order at
http://candelarianormasilva.com

Let your imagination soar!
Candelaria

Little *Stacey* loved to play

different ways on different days.

Imagination sailing free…

wondering today, what will she be?

Stacey became a frog on *Monday*,

and as a frog she hopped away.

Hopped and hopped and hopped all day,

jumped and flipped and flopped this way.

Stacey woke as a cat on Tuesday,

and as a cat she napped all day.

Napped and napped and napped all day,

stretched and yawned and purred this way.

When will she be a kid again

and get to play with all her friends?

Stacey turned into a dog on *Wednesday*,

and as a dog she barked all day.

Barked and barked and barked all day,

yelped and chased her tail this way.

Stacey woke as a pig on Thursday,

and as a pig she oinked all day.

Oinked and oinked and oinked all day,

squealed and rolled and grunted this way.

When will she be a kid again

and get to play with all her friends?

Stacey turned into a horse on Friday,

and as a horse she galloped away.

Galloped and galloped and galloped all day,

trotted and pranced and leaped this way.

Stacey became a bird on Saturday,

and as a bird she flew away.

Flew and flew and flew all day,

flapped and swooped and chirped this way.

When will she be a kid again

and get to play with all her friends?

I wonder what Stacey will be tomorrow

A frog or a cat?

She's already been that.

A dog or a pig or something really big?

Let's turn the page to see.

Stacey woke as herself on Sunday,

and as herself she went out to play.

Played and played and played all day,

played with her friends and decided to stay…

A Girl

A Girl

A Girl!

ABOUT THE AUTHOR:

Candelaria Norma Silva writes stories, essays, and blog posts inspired by her upbringing in the rich Southern soil of a large extended family in St. Louis, Missouri. She remembers learning to read after being plopped into first grade knowing only the alphabet and colors.

Soon becoming an insatiable reader, young Candelaria checked out as many books as possible from the neighborhood library each week. She still loves to read, with a special focus on reading and collecting children's books that portray children of color.

At an early age, writing chose Candelaria. That process provided a way to make sense of events in her family and neighborhood, as well as those inspired by the books she read. Her experiences as a mother and grandmother have given this author many stories to write!

Candelaria Norma Silva lives in the Dorchester neighborhood of Boston, Massachusetts, with her husband. She looks forward to long summer "take-over" visits from her grandchildren. **Stacey Became a Frog One Day** is the first in a series of books featuring this character.

Made in the USA
Middletown, DE
05 March 2021